D1119979

Monster
Birds

A NAVAJO FOLKTALE

Retold by Vee Browne

Illustrated by
Baje Whitethorne

Northland Publishing

To the Native American chiefs, the Navajo Nation, the Comanche Tribe, and the indigenous peoples of all tribal nations.
"The Four Sacred Mountains are kind to my Diné People
Before me,
Below me,
Above me,
All around me.
In the ledge of the Indian Summer, the wind blows a soft whisper, Diné . . . Diné."

I appreciate Ms. Bernice "Bee" Brown for editing my manuscripts and giving me warm support in my children's books.

—V.B.

To my wife, Priscilla; my four children, Taina, Baje Jr., Davina, and Blaine Leonard; and to all who have supported me in my art.

—B.W.

Designed by Rudy J. Ramos
Manufactured in Hong Kong by Wing King Tong

8-93/10M/0428

Author's Note   Tell this sacred story in the winter. Our Navajo legends are told only in the winter season, when the Spider People are asleep in their cocoon. If their stories are told any other season, they will be awake to hear them, and they may get angry and use their webs to wrap the storyteller. My Navajo People *(Diné)* say the time to stop telling stories is the day after the First Lightning (February 2nd of each year).

Editor's Note   This book represents one portion of the traditional Navajo story of the Hero Twins. The Monster Birds are one of four types of monsters who plague the Anasazi villages. The twins' encounter with another monster, Walking Giant, is portrayed in the book *Monster Slayer.*

Long before recorded time, there lived the Twins, Monster Slayer and Child Born of Water. They were the sons of Changing Woman and had earned honor by slaying the Walking Giant. Monster Slayer had earned his name, for it was his lightning arrow that slew the giant.

But there were still two Monster Birds who preyed upon the people of the Anasazi village. This caused the people to cry day and night. The Twins' father, Sunbearer, gave his sons the most powerful weapons on earth—the lightning arrows and magic feathers—so they could protect their people from the Monster Birds.

One day, before Sunbearer rode his turquoise horse across the sky, the Twins began their journey in the darkness of dawn. They walked to the north, up and around the plateau, and down the rolling hills of red sandstone. They came upon the butte of Shiprock, where the Monster Birds lived. This was the day the Twins planned to kill the great birds so that the village people could plant their cornfields and tend their peach orchards once again.

As the Twins walked along the valley, a giant Monster Bird appeared in the sky. The Twins looked at each other. Monster Slayer said, "Hold your magic feather tightly, my brother. I see the great bird is coming our way!"

Child Born of Water answered, "I hope the Monster Bird will not pick us up."

"Do not be afraid, my brother," Monster Slayer said calmly. "We will help our people to live in peace, without fear, and they will not be taken into the sky by this giant bird."

The Monster Bird flew in circles overhead and lowered her flight with each circle. Finally, she flew by swiftly and attempted to snatch the Twins from the earth. Monster Slayer said boldly, "She didn't snatch us this time!"

His brother said, "We must keep an eye on the talons. The giant bird's talons are strong and sharp!"

Once more the Monster Bird flew overhead, swooped down, and missed the boys. They watched her talons carefully, for they knew these could tear not only their buckskin clothing but also their flesh. As the Monster Bird flew overhead a third time, she dived down at the boys and missed again.

Monster Slayer said, "Be ready, my brother, because she may not miss us this time around."

"I will try to hit her with my lightning arrow!" Child Born of Water said as he shot his arrow—and missed!

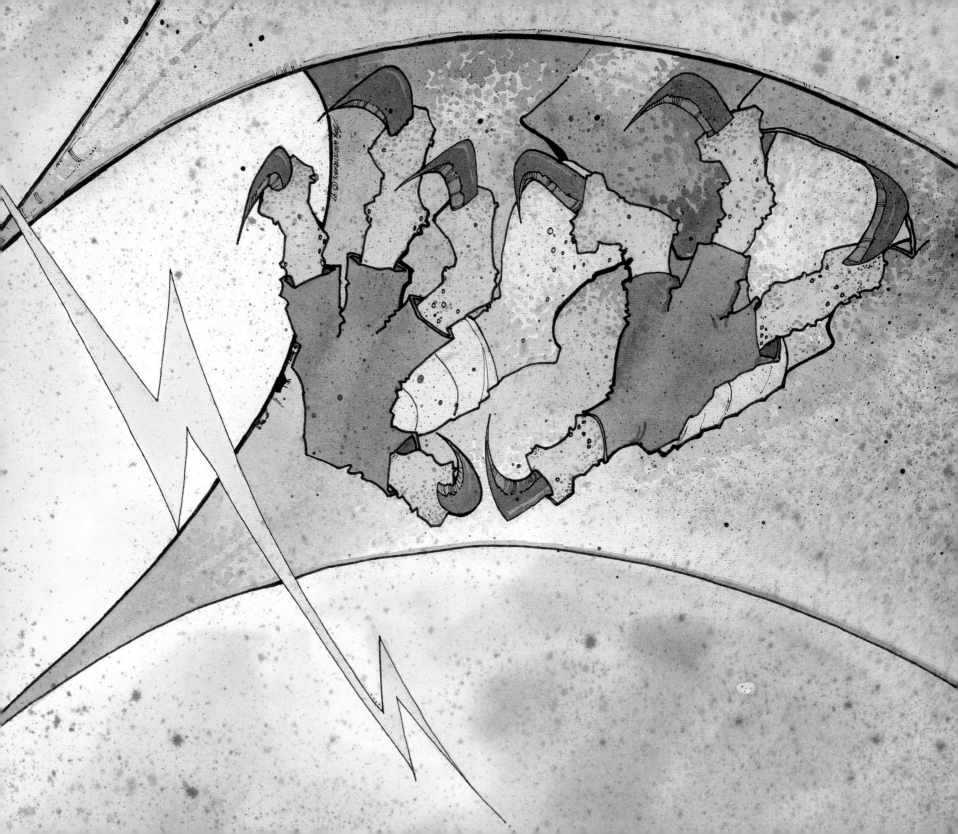

A fourth time the Monster Bird flew straight at them, and this time she snatched the Twins with her sharp talons and carried them into the sky. The Twins knew that the giant bird lived on top of Shiprock. The giant bird carried them toward Shiprock, flying higher and higher into the sky. Child Born of Water said, "If Monster Bird decides to drop us from here, we'll be safe. We have our magic feathers to protect us from harm."

Monster Slayer cried, "Look! I see a nest on top of the butte. It must be the Monster Birds' nest."

The Monster Bird carried the Twins to her nest, which held a pair of fledglings. Suddenly Monster Bird dropped the Twins from high over the butte, but the Twins used their Magic Feathers to land safely on the enormous, woven, cluttered nest. There they lay upon the twigs, pretending they were dead.

Monster Bird swooped down to her nest and told her young ones, "I have brought you something to eat!"

Instantly, the baby Monster Birds wobbled over to the Twins. But just as they were about to peck at the boys, the Twins said, "Sh . . . sh . . . shh," to the fledglings.

That startled the baby birds and they backed off. They cried, "Mama! Mama! They are not dead!"

The mother Monster Bird chided, "Of course, they're dead! You saw me drop them from the sky."

The fledglings looked at one another and said nothing, but they would not eat.

Monster Bird said, "Father Bird and I will get you more to eat." And off she flew toward the mountain to join her companion.

Again, the fledglings looked at the Twins. The Twins told the young birds, "We promise not to harm you if you can tell us when your father will return to the nest."

The fledglings squawked, "He will fly back when the Male Rain begins to pour down."

Then the Twins asked, "When will your mother return to the nest?"

They blinked and squawked, "Our mother will fly back when the Female Rain begins to pour."

The Twins waited for the young Monster Birds to settle back in their nest. "There are two types of rain," said Child Born of Water. "The Male Rain is the one that is very strong with loud claps of thunder, and the Female Rain is the one that is mild and gentle."

As soon as he said that, dark clouds emerged over the nearby mountains. The Female Rain began to pour gently. As expected, the female Monster Bird appeared through the rain. She circled in the cloudy sky, lifted her wings, and descended upon the nest.

Quickly, Monster Slayer took aim with his lightning arrow. As soon as he drew back his bow and released the arrow, Monster Bird screeched a terrible cry, "Eee . . . ck! Eee . . . ck!" The Twin's lightning arrow had hit her, and the female Monster Bird fell to earth with a loud cry. The gentle rain continued.

Again, the Twins waited, this time for the father Monster Bird. Soon the Male Rain began, accompanied by thunder and lightning. It stormed and stormed. The rain drenched the Twins and the fledglings. They shivered. A thunderbolt struck a juniper tree. At last the male Monster Bird flew through the thunderstorm to his nest, but the thunderstorm was so strong, the Twins could not see the giant bird.

"Do you see anything?" asked Child Born of Water. The Twins looked and looked.

"There he is," shouted Monster Slayer, as he took aim and released his lightning arrow. The male Monster Bird fell to earth.

True to his word that no harm would come to the fledglings, Monster Slayer spoke to the first little Monster Bird. "From this day on, my people will use your claws, your feathers, and other parts of you for healing purposes," he said.

The young Monster Bird listened. Monster Slayer commanded, "Come!" to the little fledgling. The bird came forward. He flapped his wings and clutched one magic feather given to him by the Twin. Then he rose high into the blue sky. He flew up, higher and higher, and then he turned into an eagle.

Next, Monster Slayer commanded "Come forward!" to the second fledgling Monster Bird. The bird came forward. The Twin said, "From this day, you will be a night creature." The bird flapped his wings. He clutched the last magic feather, flew off toward the approaching darkness, and turned into an owl.

Monster Slayer said, "Now that we have given away our only magic feathers for great purposes, how shall we climb down from this butte?"

His brother answered, "We will use our wisdom and ask our grandmother, Spiderwoman." So from high on the ledge of the butte, the boys looked and searched for Spiderwoman.

The Twins yelled from high above, "Grandmother!" They called and shouted. No answer. Spiderwoman said nothing. Maybe she was too busy mending her webs, the boys reasoned.

Spiderwoman was tall and as beautiful as a princess. She had
long fingernails and wore a colorful necklace. For a moment
she thought she heard small voices. She stopped to listen. She
could faintly hear soft cries: "Grandmother . . . Grandmother!"
Spiderwoman thought to herself, "Where are those small voices
coming from? I must go and see."

Finally, after the fourth time, she peered out from her
ancient ruin. She scurried up the towering volcanic plug and
looked everywhere. At last she found the Twins.

"*Yah-a-tah*, my beautiful grandsons," she said.

The boys shook her hand and said, "*Yah-a-tah, Grandmother.*"

The Twins told her their story about the Monster Birds who had eaten their people for many years, and that they were sent to earth to battle the monsters and bring peace to the villagers.

"How can I be of help to you, my grandsons?" asked Spiderwoman.

Monster Slayer answered quickly, "We need your help in climbing down the butte. In return, we will bring you the tail feathers from the Monster Birds."

Spiderwoman was pleased to hear that and said, "Very well, my grandsons, I shall help you down." At once, Spiderwoman took out her webs for the Twins.

As she spread out her webs, Child Born of Water asked, "Grandmother, how can these tiny strings take us down without breaking?"

Grandmother answered, "My webs are so strong, they can easily hold two boys your size. Here, test my webs. Pull on them!"

The Twins held the webs between their fingers, pulling and tugging very hard. The webs made a twanging sound, "ting . . . ting!" The Twins agreed that their grandmother's webs were very strong.

Spiderwoman chuckled and went on to say, "No one weaves finer webs than I. But wait! I must tell you one important thing before you climb into my web. Do not open your eyes as I lower you to the ground. I will sing my sacred Spider Song to empower the strength of my web, but if you open your eyes, the web will not hold you." She sang with a high-pitched voice. "May my web be strong to hold . . . it will hold."

She closed her eyes, clasped her hands together, and swayed to the soft, high-pitched melody. The Twins climbed into her web and sat with their eyes closed. Grandmother began her descent of the butte.

The Twins were anxious and could hardly wait to open their eyes. While they were still far above the ground, Child Born of Water took a quick peek. Spiderwoman scolded in an angry voice, "My web is beginning to lose its strength! I told you not to open your eyes!"

As soon as she said that, her web broke, and the boys fell out.

The Twins screamed, "We are falling! Aah . . . Aah!" And they fell upon the sand.

Child Born of Water gasped, "Oh, my! What a terrible fall!"

His brother sneered, "Thanks to you! Why did you open your eyes, anyway?" His knees hurt, and he rubbed them.

"I wanted to see how far we were from the ground!" exclaimed Child Born of Water.

They got up and walked in pain to the slain Monster Birds. Each took a tail feather and gave it to Spiderwoman, who had completed her descent to the ground. The Twins said goodbye to their grandmother.

Day and night the Twins traveled, and at last they arrived home safely at their mother's hogan on Holy Mountain. Changing Woman embraced them both as they told of their adventure to the north, for she was very proud of them. While they sat around a glowing fire, the scent of the juniper filled the hogan and seemed to say, "The people of the village will rejoice. They will live in peace and harmony, for they will fear no more monsters. The Monster Birds are gone and will never be seen again. They will only be heard about in stories."

Sunbearer looked down and loved what he saw. He thought to himself, "It was my twin sons who battled the monsters and saved the village people." After the villagers were free from all fears of monsters, they again planted their gardens and tended their peach orchards. Sunbearer saw that the corn in their fields grew, the clouds provided shade, and the Rain Gods brought water to the corn roots and the peach trees.

We still know today that is the way it was with the people who lived long ago.

Author   Vee Browne is a Navajo author, educator, and substance abuse counselor who grew up as a foster child in Mesa, Arizona, where she found solace, love, and comfort in books about Native American peoples. Today she lives in Chinle on the Navajo Reservation in northeastern Arizona. She has contributed short stories and poetry to several anthologies.

Illustrator

Baje Whitethorne is a Navajo artist based in Flagstaff, Arizona. His watercolor paintings have earned him honors at shows such as Santa Fe's Indian Market, The Heard Museum Indian Fair, and the Navajo Exhibition at the Museum of Northern Arizona. Rooted in Navajo tradition, each of his paintings contains a Navajo settlement in miniature (see below).